GREAT DAY for UP

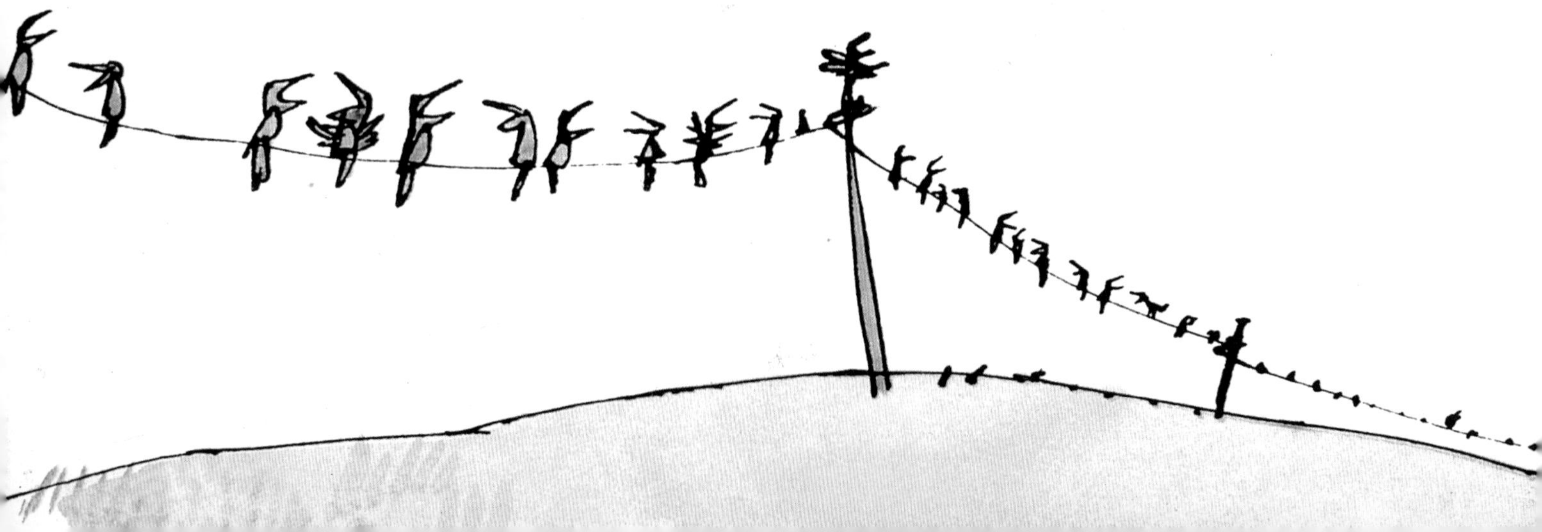

Dr. Seuss's
GREAT DAY for UP

Illustrated by
Quentin Blake

HarperCollins *Children's Books*

First published in the UK in 1975

This edition published in the UK in 2012 by HarperCollins Children's Books

HarperCollins Children's Books is a division of HarperCollins Publishers Ltd.

1 3 5 7 9 10 8 6 4 2

ISBN: 978-0-00-748753-0

Visit our website at www.harpercollins.co.uk

Printed and bound in China

UP! UP!

The sun is getting up.

The sun gets up.

So **UP** with you!

UP!

Ear number one . . .

Ear number two.

Up, heads!

Up, whiskers!

Tails!

Great day, today!
Great day
for

UP!

Up! Up!

You!
Open up
your eyes!

You worms!

You frogs!

You butterflies!

Up, whales!

Up, snails!

Up, rooster!

Hen!

Up!

Girls and women!

Boys and men!

Great day
for UP FEET!
Lefts and rights.

And **Up! Up!** Baseballs!

Footballs! Kites!

Great day
to sing
up on a wire.

UP!

Up, voices!
Louder! Higher!

Up stairs!

Up ladders!

Up on stilts!

Great
day
for up
Mt. Dill-ma-dilts.

Everybody's
doing UPs!

On bikes . . .

. . . and trees

. . . and buttercups.

Up! Up!

Waiters!

Alligators!

UP!

Up giraffes!

Great day
for seals!

Great day for UP
on ferris wheels!

UP! UP! UP!

Fill up the air.

Up, flags!
Balloons!
UP! Everywhere!

UP! UP! UP!

Great day for UP!

Wake every person,
pig and pup,
till EVERYONE
on Earth is up!

Except for me.
Please go away.
No **up.**
I'm sleeping in today.